My Rabbit's Shadow Looks Like a Hand

Rhys Hughes

My Rabbit's Shadow Looks Like a Hand
by Rhys Hughes
ISBN: 978-1-913766-05-4

Cover Art by David Rix

Publication Date: June 2021

My Rabbit's shadow
     looks like a hand
that has contorted itself in order
     to cast the shadow
of a rabbit on the wall—
a rabbit that looks just like
     the shadow of a hand
contorted to enable the casting
     of the shadow of a
          rabbit on the wall…

I yearn for a friend
     to distract my mind
          from this recursion
or else to help me enjoy it—
     a tropical woman
her shadow merging with mine
     on the moonlit stage
     of life as we peer
out of this ramshackle hutch
     called the world

My Rabbit's Shadow Looks like a Hand

I had been entertaining the children of several friends at a dinner party by casting the shadows of various animals on a wall. To make each animal I contorted my hands and the smoky yellow bulb of an old electric lamp did the rest of the work. It's a trick that many can do, but it was more common in my youth than it is now. Fashions come and go, but animals are always popular, even when they are no more than silhouettes on a flat surface. After the party I walked home.

My route took me along the river embankment and past the university on the other side. The bright windows of late study reflected themselves in the slow moving water like large square leaves that had dropped from geometrically precise trees. Or perhaps they were a new species of fish, one with riverbed shadows like delivered letters. I thought about my own student days long ago, how I had taught myself conjuring secrets from books in my free time to amuse classmates.

It was easy to astonish them with nothing more than the outline of a flapping bird on a white door, and yet the real magic all around they ignored completely. The doors of the university buildings that opened automatically as if one was a demigod held no interest for them. I softly chuckled to myself as I mounted the steps to my new abode and opened the front door. I switched on one of the many living room lights and went to prepare a final drink before bedtime.

When my hot chocolate was ready, I noticed something rather droll. The beam of the light was casting the shadow of my pet rabbit on the wall behind the pillow I had given him for a bed, and this shadow looked like a hand, like my hand in fact, a hand in the act of casting the shadow of a rabbit. An example of recursion, I asked myself? The rabbit is my most popular animal shape, of course, and it is one of the easiest to simulate. But there was something more here.

My rabbit was eating a carrot and the shadow of the carrot looked like a pen in the fingers of the hand. I wondered if my rabbit's shadow had turned into a writer's hand and it occurred to me to cast the shadow of a piece of paper, like a square fish, next to the tip of the shadow of the pen. But shadow words on shadow paper are unreadable. Far better to position a real sheet of paper under the carrot, then go to bed and discover the next morning what might be written there.

That's what I did and these are the words I found:

> Our lives are bounded by invisible
> walls we can see beyond but not
> reach through. The vistas of distance
> compel us to dream futile dreams
> and entertain fanciful notions
> that are never really entertained
> but demand their money back.
>
> I am the shadow of a rabbit but
> flatness has its trials and tribulations
> no less than solid life. It is not always
> funny to be a one dimensional bunny
> believe it or not. I might just be a slip
> of a notional thing but days are tough
> for me and nights are even worse.
>
> In this modern century of ours there
> are few people willing to notice what
> is right beneath their feet. Often it is a
> harmless shadow trodden on without

remorse. I have tales to tell about
our kind, the neglected shades of your
world, if you care to read them...

I do care and after I woke up and discovered this text I was very eager to receive the next instalment. I assumed that I would have to repeat the routine with my rabbit and that is exactly what I did in the evening. But I obtained a longer carrot with more shadow ink inside it. And in order to strengthen and clarify the shadow I decided to use the beam of a powerful torch instead of the wall lights.

The marvel (I daren't say 'miracle') of the communication from the shadow of my rabbit reminded me of something but I couldn't put my finger, or even the shadow of my finger, on what exactly it was. This bothered me a lot in the days to come. But it's not yet those days, so let's put the question aside for the time being. I went to bed as usual and when I awoke I found more words.

But they were written in a different style and it seemed that this text issued from a quite different personality.

How could this be?

Indeed, how can anything be?

You humans are quite absurd. I look at you and wonder how you arrived in the universe. Are you some kind of joke or other? I'm not exaggerating or trying to be rude for the sake of simple fun. The main ridiculousness of your condition is the fact you are vertical creatures that stroll or shuffle or hobble around on two legs and look like walking pencils, and this strikes me as so very daft. Walking like a gorilla looks fine. If you had four legs like a centaur that would be fine too. But an erect back and your vertical alignment! It definitely seems to me that you evolved from pencils rather than from apes. This sounds light-hearted but I promise you it's not at all. I genuinely find you to be disturbingly bizarre at times. You form a right angle with a snake. Two humans and two snakes could make a very nice picture frame but what picture would want to be inside it?

This statement had a much more forthright and brusque tone than the wry message of the night before. I couldn't believe the authors were the same. I thought about it and a solution came to me. Sometimes we go in search of answers but on occasion an answer comes tumbling into the open arms of our imagination. The torch had cast a different class of shadow to that thrown by the wall light. Yes, that was it.

My rabbit's shadow had still resembled a hand and the carrot was still a pen, but the angle of the torch had been different and thus it was not the same hand and the same pen as before.

This second communication had issued from a new rabbit's shadow, a shadow more forceful in character than that of the first. It occurred to me that by altering the distance and strength and angle of the light source, an exchange of information might be facilitated between myself and the full range of possible shadow rabbits. Some of these shadows would be more amusing than others, of course, but that's true of all species. I resolved to create as many hands as I could manage.

That evening I fed another carrot to my rabbit, positioned the piece of paper where it ought to be, and turned on the torch. The next day I woke early and hastened to see what was there.

You live in an interesting house
full of nooks and crannies
where the ghosts of grannies and
crooks linger still. On the dusty
windowsill I met the phantom
of a finger that moved and wrote
in the dust these solemn words:

'I was chopped off when the
window was slammed by the wind
ow! And here I have lain since,
waiting for the rest of me to return
but I don't think it has noticed the
loss. I have been damned because
I sinned, but how I know not.'

Finger, said I, you might have been
a thief in your former state, a picker
of locks unseen at night. 'I recall
picking noses but that's all,' it wrote,
'and I don't think that's quite enough
for fate to hate me the way it does.'
And I was forced to concur with this.

'There is a compensation,' it added
after a pause, as I licked my paws, 'for
I seem to be an advanced modern
finger fitted with the latest features,
doubtless a circumstance based on
the fact I lack a face, for features go
(so it's said) where they can and must
do their best in any given situation.'

How curious to hear, called I in reply, and
what might those features be? Before these
words were out of my mouth, 'Predictive
text,' it scrawled, 'and that's how I knew
you were going to ask that; it's the proof of
the pudding, as they say.' How marvellous,
a talent worth exploiting, and then I sighed.

For puddings are mostly unknown to
the taste buds of rabbits and a grass mélange
in a wide glass bowl is a treat I hanker
for with passion, yet it is never the fashion
and never a habit for restaurateurs to serve
a sample of anything divine to a hungry
example of our kind. And this is because
nobody wants to hear anyone bawl:

'Waiter! a bunny is stuffing his tummy' even if
the food is not actually theirs. But I digress, let
us return to the subject at hand, the predictive
powers of that amazing finger. An index finger
that consulted itself when it wanted to find out
the page numbers of the other fingers and also
the thumb. Never forget the thumb. I inquired:

What do you think might occur next with
so many different rabbits invited into this
house night after night? Without a fidget
the finger that was not fickle wrote, 'I am
no Seer or Sybil and do not describe futures
in the form of riddles, so I will tell you clear.'
Go right ahead, I urged that prodigal digit.

'There can only ever be twelve shadows of
rabbits summoned to appear in total,' it wrote,
'and that limit can never be exceeded, so your
master needs to heed it and make the most of
each.' At this I grew indignant and declared he
was no master over me, merely the abode owner,
a solid three dimensional duffer and no saint.

Rather abashed by my outburst the finger
curled up like a worm. That will teach you to
assume in a room, I said, when you're dead
and just a ghost, your host is not a man to be
trifled with and now we're back to desserts.
I do have more to say about this caper but I
seem to have run out of paper, so I will bid
you farewell until the next time if ever…

This poem was written in very small script on
the piece of paper and so it occurred to me
that in future I ought to provide more sheets
than one. The next rabbit's shadow might have
even more to say. From now on I would leave

a notebook and the pen could write as much as it liked. I considered it interesting that only twelve rabbits would ever show themselves to me in this manner. Three had come and gone already. I had to make the most of the nine that would follow, but how does one fuss shadows? It seems a task beyond the empathy of anybody.

The situation I was in reminded me a little of a book I had read when I was younger, *Watership Down*. But no, it wasn't at all like that really. Plus, I couldn't remember any incidents of that story in detail. I concluded that a ship made from water had no option but to go down, for it would come apart instantly and mingle with the sea and be drawn into the convection currents that plunge deep to the seabed. Whimsies of this kind frequently assail me. I was impatient for night to come. I twiddled my thumbs many times and I might have twiddled those belonging to other people had they let me. But luckily that never happened.

Never forget the thumb indeed! What a wise saying.

My communion with the shadow rabbits was the highlight of my day. I decided that to increase the chances of receiving a more substantial text to enjoy, a stronger rabbit than the previous three was required. A rabbit capable of writing more. When the time came, I moved the torch closer to its target. The shadow was bigger as a result and denser and clearer and firmer, a stocky silhouette with obvious musculature. I gave it a carrot of unusual length and went to bed satisfied.

The outcome was a prose story and I was vindicated.

The Escape

I sit at the bottom of a narrow valley, so narrow we might even call it a chasm, but in fact there is no 'we' for I am alone. I am often alone. What am I doing here? I am not sure but it doesn't matter.

It's a very peaceful place and that is enough and the steep sides of the mountains are covered with flowers. My mouth waters as I gaze upon them. That's not the only thing that waters, for there is a cool stream here that flows silently and is very blue.

I know it is cool because I drank from it just a few minutes ago. Now I wish to rest, but there is an agitation in my soul too. I am sitting but my eyes are restless and they suffer a deeper thirst.

So I gaze intently at my surroundings and attempt to slake the thirst of my eyes on what I can see. The chasm is inaccessible, that much is clear, and I don't understand how I climbed down here.

The walls of rock on either side are almost sheer and a lack of handholds means that even a seasoned climber might think twice about making the attempt. I have only one brain so I only think once.

But that is sufficient. No, I am not capable of scaling those smooth walls. I must have come along the floor of the valley, perhaps through a tunnel under the ground. Who knows? And why worry?

I look directly upwards and I see a ribbon of blue sky and it fascinates me. I forget that I am worried. Why was I so worried? It's because I didn't see my reflection in the stream when I drank from it.

Odd that such a small thing troubled me but now I am troubled no longer. Gazing at the sky has made me forget everything unpleasant. I am mesmerised by the view, by that ribbon of dazzling blue.

It seems to me that I am gazing down on a river and because of this illusion I experience slight vertigo but I am enthralled and feel weightless too. Yes, the walls of the chasm are steep and smooth.

Then something incredible happens, but it can't really be incredible because I believe it immediately. My reflection appears in this river. You may say it is a cloud but I know it's my reflection.

Fluffy, white and buoyant, just as I am. Yet there is a peculiarity about it. I blink and look more carefully. It is changing shape, the way clouds do, but it's not a cloud because I'm gazing down, not up.

This isn't the sky anymore, so it can't be a cloud, and what lives in rivers apart from reflections? I blink again and now I understand that I am gazing at a large fish, a dazzlingly white bulbous fish.

If my reflection looks like a fish, then I am a fish. It is unreasonable to believe anything else. Logic dictates and we are its secretaries. I am a fish. I shake my head, close my eyes again, tighter this time.

When I open my lids I stop gazing upwards. My neck is a little sore now. Reality returns to normal. I am at the base of a narrow valley and I'm stuck here. There's no way out for me. I'm trapped.

Then I reason to myself that if I am a fish, which is a proven fact, I can jump into the stream and swim away until I am out of the chasm. What a perfect solution! There is no need for any doubts.

I leap and bound and splash into the stream and I feel the cold waters of freedom surround me like a suit of uncomfortable but very clean clothes. Then the current is bearing me along at a fabulous rate.

My velocity increases and everything becomes a blur. I am only dimly aware of the smooth pebbles on the bed of the river beneath me and the weeds that wave farewell and bon voyage as I pass them.

A wild joy enters me and I laugh silently, bubbles erupting from my mouth and nostrils. But I soon stop accelerating and then gradually I slow down. The stream has flowed out of the valley.

The hills on either side are gentle and low now, but still festooned with flowers. I rise to the surface of the water and look directly upwards. The river that is the sky had broadened considerably.

My reflection is still there, but it is no longer a fish, it is changing again and I wonder if maybe it really was a cloud all along. I feel sure that's what you believe. It transforms itself dramatically.

Two long ears emerge from the main bulk and a cute little nose seems to twitch. A rabbit, yes that's what I am! I reach the bank and pull myself out. I am sodden but I will soon dry in the sunlight.

I have managed to escape my prison. I must have fallen into that awful chasm or maybe a cruel man hurled me there. I slid down one of the steep mountainsides and was lucky not to be killed.

The profusion of flowers helped to break my fall. But now I am ravenous. On the softly undulating crests of these much lower hills I stand and nibble a flower. Then I nibble another. And another.

How many flowers can you nibble? Not as many, I bet! You are not a rabbit, but I am. This is the way I prefer it to be. Now I will rest underneath the uneaten flowers and wait for evening.

I smiled and sighed, for I too had little more to do than wait for evening. I knew for certain, however, that I wasn't a rabbit. Moving the torch closer had made a strong shadow with a stronger personality but there was still a great deal of wistfulness mixed with the strength. More experiments were needed. I thought about positioning two torches a certain distance apart to throw a pair of shadows on the wall.

That might be a worthwhile approach, because both shadows might be different in temperament even though projected from the same rabbit. It would be a scientific opportunity to settle the old question, 'Do identical twins always behave the same way?'

Yet I was made acutely aware of the dangers of obsession. I needed to be engaged with ordinary life as well as with my shadow adventures. So I made a determined effort to leave my house and be sociable. I am invited to parties regularly. Lately I had been declining to attend. I still wasn't in the mood to blend with crowds of human beings, but it wouldn't harm me to meet one or two nice individuals and indulge in pleasant talk. I went to the café where Belinda often sat alone.

She was there today too, out on the terrace in the sun and drinking an elaborate concoction of coffee, chocolate, coconut milk, vanilla pods and other spices in a tall glass. Her bicycle was leaning against the railings. It was upside down and this detail struck me as odd. But I supposed she had been fixing a puncture on one wheel.

She smiled when she saw me and said, "Bonjour."

I loved her accent and felt soothed by her chestnut honey eyes and her black hair that was like an eruption of springs from a clockwork volcano. I sat next to her and shrugged at the bicycle. I saw that blank white cards had been threaded through the spokes.

"That's what I used to do when I was young," I said, "because I liked the noise they made as they span."

"Yes, like they were being shuffled by a robot."

"Yours aren't playing cards."

"This is a different kind of experiment."

"Will you show me?"

She nodded and stood, elegant as music, melodiously made her way to the inverted bicycle and turned the pedals with her strong hands as if she was grinding two pepper pots simultaneously. The back wheel span and the white cards flashed as they moved.

She sat back down and the sun cast her shadow onto the cards. But it wasn't direct sunlight that did this. Her glass acted like a prism and a ray of coffee-infused sunshine flavoured with coconut and spices darted from the drink and projected her outline onto the revolving screen. When the cards were stationary the effect was nothing special but now it seemed we were watching a curious film together.

The shadow was Belinda and yet it somehow wasn't.

It flickered and changed.

For an instant it turned into something strange.

An entity unknown to me…

The wheel slowed down, came to a stop.

Belinda said very calmly:

"You like to make the shadows of animals with your hands and in fact you are very good at making rabbits. Other people can do this too. I have made rabbits that way, for instance."

"There is nobody in the world who hasn't."

"But if our hands make shadow rabbits and such rabbits are no more than the projections of the hands of other beings, who in this case are us, who is to say that we ourselves aren't simply the projections of the hands of beings from another dimension?"

"A very good point, crisply made," I replied.

The waiter brought my coffee.

It was in a tall glass too and I had an idea.

With my hand I made the shadow of a rabbit on the glass, but the ears were longer than usual, and I cried:

"Waiter! Waiter! Look!"

He turned and sighed and then he said, and Belinda said at exactly the same moment, "There's a hare in my drink."

"Very good, sir," he added.

I sipped my beverage. My escape from shadows had simply led me in a metaphorical circle. I was back in the shadowlands. I knew for sure that human beings were just the three-dimensional shadows cast by the hands of four-dimensional creatures.

But what could I do about that? Not much!

I had a lot to think about as I went home and set up conditions for the night that was to come. I had bought a second torch in a shop on the way back and I did as I suggested earlier, arranging them in such a way that a pair of shadows was cast from the one rabbit.

Two sheets of paper were required.

One carrot but two pens!

The rabbit shadows weren't identical, as it happens. One was slightly smaller than the other. Getting the angles absolutely precise was beyond me, so I left it the way it was, with one hand just a little more delicate and softer in outline, and went to bed.

In the morning I found two texts on the sheets.

I give them to you side by side.

They work better that way.

My angel, my dove, my love
but you're not a winged
woman or bird, so scrap those
first two, now I gaze at you
and how I wish to sweetly kiss
your amazing paws.

After a teasing pause, just to
give you cause to sigh, I reply
with a twinkle in my eye, 'But
really, sir, we've only just met
and haven't even been properly
introduced yet.'

Love cares nothing for time,
like space it is relative, not that
we are related in the conven-
tional sense. We are in fact
variations of just one individual cast as a pair of images.

Quite an unusual chat up line
but there's something so very
fine in your bearing that I'm
inclined to give you the ben-
efit of the doubt. If I am you,
and you are me, what are we?
And where are we going?

We are narcissists, is the
answer to your query, in love
with each other and thus ourselves. Like identical elves we
have long ears, but softer furs,
and better years if you give me
a chance to serve you as a male
in olden days was expected

Hold your horses! I never said
I was in love with you…

to serve a maid. Chivalry
and romance, it is called, but
whether it comes when it's
called or not, I don't know.
My darling, please say you'll
be mine, just nod your pretty
head as a sign.

I am amused and entertained
by all you have said so far, but
that's not the same as feeling
strong desire or even a mild
affection. It would be totally
wrong if I confessed out of
the blue that your efforts to
woo me were likely to succeed.
Hold your horses, I say again.
Your need is too transparent.
You might well be a window
or a ghost for the sheerness
of your intentions. Draw the
drapes!

I have no horses. I am a
rabbit. What would a rab-
bit do with those? Horses are
for courses, of course, and I
have only pauses. I paws for
thought, a rabbit like you. A
rabbit, not an ape. A rabbit
never forces.

The shadow of a rabbit is what
you are. A shadow like a cape
discarded near the wall. As
for what you'd do with them,
plenty, is my guess. But feel no
stress or despair, because it's
only fair that I reject the bait
of your advances. A horse can
prance at any time, it's true,
but a bunny must be hope-
ful, happy and ever sunny and
should never risk a spontane-
ous date.

You are forthright, for sure!

I understand your position,
my dear, and in fact you are
quite right. There are many
dangers in this world and male
rabbits can be awful. Forgive
my impatience and imperti-
nence. Perhaps I will set off
for France to join the Foreign
Legion next week and forget
all about you. Then maybe I
will be killed in a distant land
and the hand that writes these
words no will be no more. You
will seek me in vain for I shall
be stew in the mouth of time,
chewed by doom and gloom,
a sombre tune, and you and I
will never get a room together.
But that's life. Ah well.

How melodramatic!

How absurd!

You really are a joker and the
twinkle in your eyes makes up
in part for the nonsense that
you speak. It's quite an art to
charm while being so daft at
the same time. I have softened
to you just a smidgen but in
truth I was already smitten
with the girth of your ears.

It certainly is.

Oh, happy day!

Please don't go getting ideas!
This doesn't mean I am in love
with you yet. Maybe it will
happen, maybe not. My

I hope it does.

I am, my dearie and thank you
sincerely.

Your lips are divine and I
think it most fine that you
should employ them in such
a manner. They render your
face even more sultry than it is
already. My own are ready.

I can only stammer that I'm
appreciating your aspects to a
greater and greater degree as
the seconds pass, so let them
pass as quick as they can.

Oh yes, please!

doubts are large and you can't
hope to barge them aside with
your pride and smarm and
your old fashioned romantic
bluster. I trust you are quite
clear on that, buster?

Now that has all been sorted
out tell me how do you like
my pout?

Employ? Employ!

Employ?!

My lips aren't employed, good
sir, they volunteer for every
mission. Now let's consider
what we can do to pass the
time, for the night is still
young and dawn is far away.
Forget the day to come. We
have the velvet dark on which
to rest our hearts. It's time to
make a start.

A love story, clearly, and I realised I was in danger of being overrun with little shadows if these two amorous rabbits ever managed to meet and do what all rabbits do when given the opportunity, which is to breed. I would end up with a house so murky that I shouldn't see its interior again, for no artificial light is powerful enough to cut through layers and layers of baby rabbits, dozens of overlapping shadows gambolling everywhere, piling up in all the corners like animated treacle.

I decided never to repeat the experiment with two torches. One rabbit at a time is easier and safer. I spent the rest of the day thinking deeply on what Belinda had said. Maybe she and I were just variant shadows of the same inexplicable hand from the fourth-dimension? I didn't know if the notion pleased or repulsed me. To be closer to Belinda would be superb, of course, and very handy in that manner, but it would also be a nuisance to know we had no separate existence.

Also there was a speck of terror in the eye of the idea.

I will endeavour to explain why.

Our hand casts the shape of a rabbit on the wall only when that hand is contorted unnaturally. If Belinda was right and we ourselves were little more than the shadows of alien hands, it meant that our forms were those of contorted hands too, that our shapes were unnatural, that if we wanted to know what those alien hands actually looked like we should uncurl our bodies, but to us it would seem we were twisting them oddly. I wondered if yoga practitioners guess any of this?

Well, there is little use worrying about such things.

So I went out to buy carrots.

The grocer who owns the shop at the end of my road likes to joke on the topic of my sudden fondness for that particular vegetable. In the past few days I had only bought carrots from him. He thought I was trying to fix my eyesight or turn myself orange. His speculations in this regard had no great originality about them. Today I revealed to him that rabbits were consuming them, not me, and he said:

"Rabbits are fine animals. My favourite book—"

"*Watership Down*? Yes, but how could any ship made from water stay afloat? It would plop itself down, melt away, disperse on the ocean waves and currents, dissolve itself forever."

I felt smug with my retort, but he answered:

"Not if it was made from ice, for that's water too and keeps its shape, and in fact plans were once drawn up for a vessel constructed from ice, a vast ship, an aircraft carrier, but it was never built. This has nothing much to do with rabbits, but I don't mind changing the subject, for I'm a grocer and change is an everyday part of our world. We see produce alter as the hours wear on. It wilts and saddens."

In the aftermath of this speech I felt compelled to offer him my hand for a shake. What a unique grocer! Now my mind would be filled with an armada of icy ships crewed by rabbits.

But what sort of rabbits would feel at home on such a vessel? Polar rabbits, I imagine. How might I make one of those? A colder light could be the answer. Different kinds of bulbs in my torch would produce light of varying qualities and textures, but whether the nature of the shadows casts by those bulbs would also be different remained to be seen. Well, I thought there could be no harm in trying.

There is never harm in trying until it has been tried...

I had my carrots in my shopping bag.

So I went to the hardware store and bought a frosty bulb, the coldest they had in stock. I was assured by the shopkeeper that it made a light as hard as an icicle but with a blue tinge.

My final visit was to the cafe where Belinda was just setting off for a ride on her bicycle. I remembered what the shadow of the lovesick male rabbit had said to the shadow of the coy female rabbit, and I deliberately said nothing to her even remotely like any of that. I didn't even run after her to stop her from departing from me.

Belinda, caramel and golden in the afternoon sun, riding away with kinky curls bobbing and a wave to me. Her smile a white sunbeam with nothing cold in it despite the fact that white is the hue and cry of snow. I ordered an espresso and swallowed it.

Back in my apartment I screwed the new bulb into the torch and when night came, I fed a carrot to my rabbit, arranged the sheets of paper in the correct position and projected the beast's shadow. I was an expert bunny shadow projector now. The shadow was all umbra with no penumbra to fuzzy the clarity.

A warm night, relatively speaking, but an icy light. And I went to bed and shivered under my own sheet, cotton rather than paper, with shiverings of longing, not coldness.

The result in the morning was certainly interesting.

> Captain of the *Habakkuk* I was,
> a frozen watership, a big boat
> with a hull of ice. Afloat on the
> waves of the northern sea, a berg
> with straight edges and a cabin
> for me. But should ever a rabbit
>
> have to endure such conditions?
> Falling snow made me groan so.
> Ought ever a fluffy bunny with
> languorous eyes be exposed to the
> harm of the chill Arctic skies?
>
> I thought not and said as much in
> a letter to the Admiralty. The Sea
> Lords discussed my epistle while
> drinking rum-laced tea for free and
> soon concluded I was unfit to rule
>
> the men under my thumb, the crew
> of goose pimples that manned the
> vessel like erect hairs on an arm.
>
> Always right and very wise they
> relieved me of my command and
> ordered me to sail back to land...

Captain's Log. Day One of the Mutiny. I refuse to remain in the far north. I also decline to return to land and be arrested. This means that only one course of action is left open to me. I must become a rebel, an outcast, a pirate. Will my men stay loyal to me? This is the question that presently concerns me the most. Then I remember that they aren't men but goosebumps. If I offer them a raise I am sure I can count on them. One, two, three! Like beads on an abacus of frights, that's how they are. I will tell them a ghost story or two. That will stiffen their resolve and forms. It's the only raise I can offer them.

Captain's Log. Day Two. The men are with me. They also hate the long working hours that the Admiralty impose. Up at dawn every morning and no bed before midnight. I will be tolerant of their wishes in this regard and improve conditions for them. They will soon grow to love me. They won't oppose my plans to head south and sail into warmer waters. *Habakkuk* was a prophet but there's no profit in remaining in the north. I want to see coconuts floating past rather than ice-floes. What are we doing at this high latitude anyway? Observing the *aurora borealis,* bathing in its eerie green flicker.

Captain's Log. Day Six. The last three entries of this log were erased by an enormous wave that broke over the side of the ship and swept into my cabin. The salt water made the ink run and my words and the brine eloped together. I haven't seen my words since. No matter! We are on our way to the tropics. Full steam ahead! And 'steam' is the key word here. I want to sail along the humid jungles of the equatorial zone, hugging the coasts on which they are found, the same way I'd like to hug my friends, if I had any, if I had arms. The goosebumps are told a fresh ghost story every night before bed.

> Further south every day, on our way
> to the balmy isles. I'm not barmy for
> wanting this. I'm sure the Admiralty
>
> are after me, seeking *Habakkuk* with
> their submarines, seeing me in their
> dreams as a bunny bogyman. Mutiny
>
> is not their cup of tea, it doesn't taste
> of rum, that's why. I would rather die
> than be forced to go back north into
>
> the frost. For at what cost to my soul?
> We zigzag our way across the waves
> and I wave hello to the dignity that
>
> awaits my arrival on a platform of the
> station of bliss. I wouldn't miss this for
> gold or pearls, oh no, because it means

the whole world to me. Wait and see!
Well, the whole world apart from all
the frozen bits. You can keep those...

Captain's Log. Day Fifteen. Every morning I
take a stroll around the deck of this mighty
vessel and I have noticed something odd.
My strolls take less time each day and I'm
wondering if I am getting fitter, if my muscles
have expanded, if the full circuit of the ship
is no longer much of a walk at all for me.
Yet I don't feel especially muscular. It must
be psychological. When we are worried, our
worlds contract and make us feel we are
being squeezed by reality. I am worried even
though I am happier than I have been for a
long time. I am worried my happiness won't
last, that the Admiralty will intercept us.

Captain's Log. Day Thirty. It's no mirage or
trick of the mind. The ship really is shrinking!
We are now in the vicinity of the island of
Bermuda, heading for the Caribbean and
then who knows where? Maybe Brazil or
across the ocean to Africa. But I measured
the length of the deck last night and it's now
only half of what it's supposed to be. Have
sharks been nibbling parts of the hull? Are
frogmen employed by the Admiralty stealing
chunks as we proceed? I am concerned
for another reason. Crew members are
missing. Originally there were one thousand
goosebumps. Now there are only 666.

Captain's Log, Day Forty. Of course I knew all along that as the climate grew warmer the goosebumps would be danger of vanishing, for what is a goosebump but a manifest reaction to the cold? Yet I thought my ghost stories would keep all of them intact by providing a different kind of chill. Clearly my stories aren't effective enough. The ship is dissolving around me and my men are deserting and my plans are falling apart. There are no lifeboats on this vessel. I mean, there were lifeboats but I broke them up for ice when I was making cocktails. I drink a large *caipirinha* every night before bed.

> Goosebumps, where are you? Why
> did you leave me alone? The voyage
> is lonely and I'm so far from home.
> My hutch is three thousand leagues
> hence and there's nothing to eat. No
>
> lettuce or beetroot, cabbage or kale,
> carrots or ripe fruit, and the only loot
> this pirate has seen is the drifting
> root of a large tree on which stood a
>
> mute gull. Woe is me! I want my tea
> and my supper too. I might even try
> eating a goosebump if any remained.
> I suspect they taste like gooseberry
> fool. But I'm not a ghoul. I wouldn't.

Captain's Log, Day One Hundred and One. It was inevitable that a ship made from ice would begin to melt when it reached warmer waters and that there would be almost nothing left of it by the time it was within the equatorial zone. But I'm no fool. *Habakkuk* is not just frozen water. There is wood pulp mixed in with the ice. It was proven by the scientists of the Admiralty long ago that the wood pulp would prevent the ice from melting. I expected to be able to sail the warm seas for many years. But now it seems I have been deceived. No doubt corners were cut when the ship was being constructed.

Captain's Waterlogged Log. The wood pulp was left out of the mix, I'm sure of it, and someone in the Admiralty pocketed the extra cash for its provision. Oh, rank humanity! I must abandon ship, but how? Perhaps I can write a message and place it in a bottle and cast the bottle over the side? The message will ask for help in a hurry. But no, that will take too long. What alternatives are there? Then I am inspired. I know exactly what to do. I will roll up my shadow and put it in the bottle instead. My shadow is my essence, my spiritual matter. Maybe I will be adopted by a friendly current and taken somewhere.

I read this account over breakfast and my spoon tinkled on the side of my cereal dish like an icicle snapping, and goosebumps ran up the length of my eating arm. I wondered if they were the same goosebumps that had fled the shrinking ship? I tried to shake them off but without success. The only thing that worked was to fully unroll my shirt sleeve. That persuaded them to return to wherever they'd come from. I decided that the cold light experiment had been worth conducting.

But I had no intention of repeating it. I would replace that frosty bulb and maybe substitute a much warmer one for the next occasion. While I finished my breakfast with a second cup of coffee, the postman delivered some letters through the flap in my door.

I examined them. Among the bills, there were invitations to parties. I was still valued as an entertainer of children. I knew what they were even without opening them. They always come in colourful envelopes. I was about to sadly throw them all aside when I realised that one of them was from Belinda. How excited I was now!

It never occurred to me to wonder how she knew my address, nor how I recognised her handwriting. I guess these things just happen. And I tore open the envelope and read her message.

I was surprised by how breathless I felt, as if I had just swum the river to reach the university on the opposite bank, as once I did for a dare, but a dare that I dared myself. The most absurd kind. Belinda had invited me to a party, yes, but not to entertain children. Nonetheless she hoped I would make the shadows of rabbits on the wall.

I felt I was capable of doing that for her, and I smiled.

Then I saw that the place of the party was my own apartment and that nobody else was invited. I had to read the message three times before the significance of this sunk into my brain.

Was Belinda asking me for a date in an oblique way?

Inviting herself around for dinner?

Some people might regard that as forward, but forward is exactly the way I wanted to go. I would just have to ensure that I cooked a meal tasty enough to do justice to her company. I already had in mind a tagine with pomegranate seeds sprinkled on top.

What should I offer her to drink? I had no idea.

No matter. I would decide later.

In the meantime I set off to find a new bulb for my torch. I say 'in the meantime' but in fact there was nothing mean about that time at all. It was sunny and rosy, a time that glowed all around me in every moving thing. I walked with a spring in my step, then I wondered where the spring had come from, from a bed or a clock, or perhaps it was one of Belinda's stray hairs, curled up tight, a helix down which my sighs might slide. The only thing I knew for sure was that the replacement bulb had to be a warm one, no frozen white light, no more chills.

In the hardware store I purchased a red bulb.

A pale but optimistic red, not the hue of rich blood or dark lipstick. A red closer to the blush of sunrise an instant before the highest point of the sun's disc lifts over the eastern horizon.

Not that I'm often up early enough to enjoy the sunrise glow. I tend to linger in bed. But I've made the effort occasionally. My facts are accurate. The new bulb was dimmer than the white ones and the shadow it cast was of diminished clarity. What would the result be? I had long forgotten my resolution to provide a notebook instead of a single piece of paper, and on this occasion the sheet I rested against the tip of the shadow of the carrot pen was a square blank one, unlined.

It had been torn from a sketchpad I never used.

The result in the morning was:

I was surprised, but really there was no need for such a reaction. There's no good reason why a shadow rabbit shouldn't be a visual artist instead of a poet or prose writer. This drawing was a little risqué, true, but that's not unusual in the art world. The bulb had been red, so what else could I have reasonably expected? It was some kind of fin-de-siècle scene, perhaps set in a bordello for rabbits, probably located somewhere in France. Yes, that seemed highly likely. A sketch by a rabbit version of Toulouse-Lautrec. I took the sheet and taped it to the mirror.

Very French. I must point out that Belinda isn't French, although she speaks the language fluently. She's from Mauritius. As for myself, I have always been a dullard when it comes to learning languages and that's why I took so eagerly to making gestures and then proceeded from gestures to the creation of shadow animals. Fingers are my substitute for tongues. I better understand the syntax of shadows.

My mind was whirling now. I decided to look for the bookshop at the heart of the city that sold almost any book one might want.

No one knew how many titles it had in stock in total, not even the owners. On a whim I intended to buy a copy of *Watership Down*. It was time to read it again, to refresh my memory about that epic story.

The shop is actually a cave in the side of the mountain that dominates the city. The city was constructed around that mountain, but the mountain is riddled with tunnels and pocked with caverns, some natural and others artificial. The bookshop looks like a normal shop from the front, then one opens the door and steps through into a weird subterranean world of rock formations, stalactites, phosphorescent pools, and towers of books, piled on each other randomly. One wanders for hours in the eerie glow, peering at faded covers, trying to decipher titles.

When I entered I discovered that I was alone there. Maybe the staff had wandered off into the deeper regions. I browsed but the books were never stacked in any order. It was a case of allowing pure chance to be one's guide. It goes without saying that a customer rarely finds the book they are seeking, but nearly always finds a substitute as good or better. I couldn't find what I'd come in for, but I did snare a first edition copy of *Archy and Mehitabel*, that marvellous romp by Don Marquis, a work that is joyous and mournful at the same time.

I thumbed my way through it and in the greenish glow I read poems I had forgotten but now easily remembered. Archy is a cockroach with the soul of a human poet. He has been reincarnated into a body that is rather inconvenient for him. Mehitabel is a cat who claims to be a reincarnation of Queen Cleopatra. Archy is only able to communicate by jumping onto the keys of an old-fashioned typewriter, painfully spelling out messages in free verse on a solitary sheet of paper.

My own position with the rabbits resembled that of Don Marquis'. He received messages from a very unusual cockroach via a typewriter, and I receive messages from shadow rabbits via carrot pens. Now I knew why I felt I was in an oddly familiar situation. The earliest messages given to me had reminded me of something. It was this! I felt the relief that comes when a minor mystery has been solved.

I didn't buy the book because there was no one to buy it from. But for the remainder of the day I thought a lot about reincarnation. I went home and as the day came to an end I made preparations for the eighth message and felt perhaps a twinge of sadness that there would only be another four after this one. I was enjoying my interaction with the shadow rabbits. The companionship was odd but uplifting.

The torch cast the shadow of the rabbit on the wall, as usual, and the shadow of the carrot it was eating. Presto, the hand and pen! The sheet of paper was in position. All was exactly right, yet I noted how the rabbit's ears were a little floppy tonight. They drooped at different angles. And it seemed that the hand on the wall was indicating the time with two of its fingers. 10:40 pm. This shadow time happened to be the same as the real time and this coincidence made me pause.

Then I thought nothing more of it and retired to bed. I woke early and went to examine the new writing that had been left for me. It was not yet dawn. The torch was still casting the rabbit's shadow on the wall. The pen had been devoured hours ago but the ears of the creature were still acting like the hands of a reliable timepiece. 6:10 am. Once again, this was very accurate. How funny! It seemed the two bunny ears really had turned into the hour and minute hands of a wall clock.

They must have been slowly rotating on the fluffy head all night, one faster than the other, keeping good time while I slept upstairs. I retrieved the sheet of paper and frowned. It was covered with a scrawl so tiny I had to take it into my study to read under a magnifying glass. Why did I keep forgetting to put more than one sheet at the disposal of the shadow hands? Some hands are just more prolific than others. Anyway, this was another prose tale, but prefaced with a short verse:

Reincarnation? Yes, I can believe
in it for the duration
of this night and in fact I recall
my former life as a
human being, a man like you but not
really like you at all,
for he never tried to cast his
rabbit's shadow
on a wall.

The Package Holiday

I hadn't been sleeping well for a number of weeks and now I was dreadfully tired for most of the working day. This was a disadvantage when it came to making money because I often made mistakes instead. I don't suffer from insomnia as a rule but my bed seemed to have a mind of its own. It didn't want me to enjoy a restful night's sleep. Maybe it disliked people, you will surely say, or maybe it was haunted. But it was brand new, purchased from a furniture store near my house, and the ghost of a previous owner couldn't be the reason for the disturbance in the middle of the night that kept me from enjoying a wondrous slumber. Nor do I truly believe that beds have independent minds and malicious personalities. Also, I need to stress that my sleep was disturbed in a very subtle way, in a manner so gentle that I remained asleep while it was taking place. It just wasn't a *good* sleep, not deep or refreshing.

I would go to bed at roughly the same time every night, on the stroke of midnight or just a minute either side, and I would jump out of bed in the morning at any time between 6 o'clock and 10 o'clock. My bed is large and that's why I bought it. I don't like narrow beds, I have a fear of them, and this peculiar phobia dates from a time when I was a passenger on a ship on a very long voyage. I had a bunk only slightly wider than my body. I rolled out of it on more than one occasion and bruised myself on the hard wooden boards below, waking up the other passengers at the same time. I wasn't very popular on that journey. I vowed I would never sleep in such a small bed again, and when I started my own business I treated myself to the largest bed I could find in any shop.

It was circular and big enough for three or four people, but I had it all to myself, and I slept in the middle, with my belly button at the centre point. My head always pointed to north and I knew this because I could see the pole star through the big round window of my bedroom. My head would sink into the soft pillow and I would gradually close my eyes and drift away into sleep. It was an extremely comfortable bed, which made the later disturbances all the more annoying. These disturbances actually began immediately every time. When I say 'later' I only mean they became unbearably annoying after an hour or so. I could ignore them until then, especially when I was physically spent, as happened one recent Monday.

I had been working especially hard on that particular day. I work from home and my business involves importing cotton products from abroad and sending them to distributors in my own country. I was expecting a delivery man to arrive early the next day to pick up the latest batch. I had to prepare the boxes, filling them with the products, sealing them and then carrying the boxes down to the hallway. He wouldn't come up the stairs to fetch them. That wasn't part of his job. I had to carry them down myself, one at a time, and there were more than forty of them, all very heavy. Three flights of stairs too. I was exhausted by the time I'd finished.

But at least it was all done and now I could crawl into bed and finally relax.

I allowed my head to sink into the pillow and I only had the energy to smile at the pole star through the very clear glass before I felt myself growing lighter and lighter. And then I was oblivious of everything. But no, that's not quite right. I was aware of a very slow moving sensation, as if I was on the deck of a ship that was turning with the current, very slowly indeed. It was this sensation that I always felt when I slept in this bed and it was this sensation that eventually became irritating and prevented me from enjoying the deep sleep I craved so badly. I can't sleep properly when I am in motion. Yes, I know the world spins, that our planet revolves around the sun, but I can't feel *that* movement. You know what I mean.

The crux of the problem was that my position would change throughout the night, so that I never woke up aligned in the same direction in which I fell asleep. I liked to sleep with my head pointing to north. I would wake up with my head pointing to the east or the south or the west. It depended on what time I woke. That was the truly curious thing. If I woke at six o'clock then I would be facing due south. This meant that during the night my body had rotated by 180 degrees. My head was now where my feet had originally been. It made no sense. At least it made no sense to *me* and I was the one most directly concerned with the phenomenon, or so I felt. I know that everyone tosses and turns but this was far too mechanical.

Once, as an experiment, I stayed in bed all morning, drifting in and out of uneasy sleep, and on the stroke of noon I found that I had returned to my starting point. My head was pointing north again. I had made a full circuit of the round bed. But why? Was my subconscious trying to tell me something? Was it determined that my own tossing and turning should be more precise than that of other sleepers? I couldn't believe it. There must be an external reason, not an internal one. I was the victim of forces, not the instigator of them. But those forces were a mystery and one I doubted I could solve. Anyway, on the night of my exhausting day, with the boxes all stacked in the hall ready for the delivery man, I had a dream.

The dream consisted of nothing at all other than a pendulum that swung from side to side. It was such a boring dream that I grew impatient with it and snapped open my eyes, only to learn that I had shifted position a little. Then I would attempt to return to sleep and the pendulum would appear again and now it was so boring that it pushed me into a deeper sleep, for which I was grateful, but this was only a temporary respite. The sound of the enormous thing as it swung back and forth in my mind woke me up again. I was almost a pendulum myself, alternating between drowsy wakefulness and lucid oblivion. I felt dizzy and rhythmically unhappy. The pendulum also reminded me of an oar rowed by a maltreated slave on a galley.

You may ask why I made no effort to return to my original position through the effort of my limbs. My answer is that I lacked energy for even such a simple recourse. I was like the dial of a compass that is at the mercy of a magnet held in the hand of a mischievous child who forces it to point away from north. Assuming that children still play such tricks. I was overcome with lassitude bordering on paralysis, another reason why I refused to believe that I was rotating on the bed under my own power. No, there had to be a force acting on me. But where from? The dream persisted throughout the night. Finally, at seven o'clock in the morning, I eased myself out of bed. I was facing southwest and I was very tired indeed.

But I had to greet the delivery man when he arrived. I dressed quickly, slipped my feet into slippers and hurried down the stairs to the hallway. The boxes loomed there like the blocks of stone of an ancient temple, but a temple dedicated to some very incompetent deity. I was expecting the delivery man to be a veritable giant, a strongman, so when I heard a tapping on the front door I flung it open and looked up. There was nothing there. Just the overcast sky. Then I looked down and saw him. He was maybe six inches tall and he had a very squeaky voice. As he slipped between my legs into the hall he glanced at the boxes and said, 'All of these? You must be joking!' I shook my head and he clenched his fists in a tiny rage.

I calmly informed him that I had already paid for them to be collected this morning. 'Who do you take me for?' he cried. 'Do you think I'm Atlas?' And then he stormed back out, a very small storm in truth, a tiny dust devil. I followed him and saw that his van was in proportion to his own dimensions. A single box could probably be balanced in its roof but no more than that. 'Where are you going?' I demanded. 'Back to the depot,' he told me. Then he added, 'I hate this job,' and I was able to fully sympathise with him. 'I don't much care for mine either,' I said. We exchanged a meaningful glance. It felt very good, exquisite in fact, so we exchanged a few more. The same idea struck both of us at the same instant and we acted on it.

'Let's go on holiday instead,' I said, while he nodded his tiny head in the affirmative. I decided to forget all about my import business. He decided to forget about the depot. I straddled the roof of his van and he started the engine. We drove down the road like that and I can't say it was uncomfortable. I spoke to him and he left his window open so he might hear me. I told him about my problem with the bed. 'No mystery there at all,' he declared. 'How so?' I cried, as the wind combed my hair. 'The bedsprings in your mattress certainly came out of a clock,' he answered, and it all made perfect sense at last. 'When it comes to large and obsolete grandfather clocks,' he added, 'the internal parts are often secretly recycled.'

All that remained was to decide where we would go for our holiday. He had mentioned the mythical figure Atlas, so it occurred to me that the Atlas Mountains might be a destination worthy of our time and effort. He agreed with me and changed gear and we rumbled down the roads that snake their way to the south. Days passed and then the scent of pomegranates, apricots and the snow on the summits of very high peaks reached my nostrils. I sneezed, clearing the dust of the journey from my sunburned nose, inhaled deeply and sighed. We were nearing our destination! We had thrown it all to the winds and now the winds were delivering us, instead of all the packages I had made ready, to a land where time passed slower.

I simply couldn't believe that beds here had clock springs inside them instead of mattress springs. Such a state of affairs would be completely contrary to the tranquil mood evoked by our surroundings. Then we *saw* the mountains. They were tall and grand and rugged, of course, but more colourful than I had been expecting. They were streaked and splotched with blue, red, green, brown, white, grey, black, orange and yellow. I had to stand up to view them more respectfully, to drink in their splendour with my eyes. It wasn't easy keeping my balance on the roof of that small van on the rutted roads. In fact I fell off when we went over a bump and the little man stopped the van and got out to help me up with encouragement.

He simply wasn't strong enough to help me up with his arms! No matter. I thanked him and then I said wistfully, 'But I don't even know your name,' and he smiled and said, 'It is Salta and I'm happy to be here with you.' 'Salta is Atlas backwards,' I pointed out. 'Yes, I know,' he replied, 'and my mother gave me that name because I am so small, the very opposite of a giant who can support the sky on his shoulders.' 'And yet the sky weighs nothing,' I mused, and we smiled. We decided to complete the remainder of the journey on foot, Salta and I, to the foot of those mighty mountains. It just seemed the right thing to do. The noise of the engine wasn't appropriate to the serene environs in which we found ourselves.

Because the stones of the ground were sharp we hopped rather than walked. Little did I guess back then that one day I would be reincarnated as a rabbit! As we neared the foot of the range it became clear that these mountains weren't made of rock but some other substance. What could it be? We hurried to find out, hopping madly, and when we reached the first and touched it with reverent fingers we were both stupefied to discover they consisted of paper. Yes, paper mountains! Gigantic sheets of paper that had been crumpled up into peaks. More than this, we understood that these sheets were in truth pages from a colossal atlas. They were maps, all of them. 'Which is why it is called the Atlas Range,' we said wisely to ourselves.

We climbed a little way up one of the less steep gradients for the sheer joy of ascension, Salta and I, and it became clear as we rose higher that the map we were climbing was a map of my own country. The adjacent mountains were crumpled maps of France, Italy, Madagascar, Japan, Borneo, Bolivia, Cuba, Estonia and Latvia, Tasmania, and the Islands of the Pacific. I sat on a crease to catch my breath and dangled my legs over the void. 'I was never suited for a job as a delivery man,' Salta said as he sat next to me. 'You just aren't strong enough,' I agreed. He digested this, nodding. 'I wonder what the time is?' he asked next. 'How can we tell?' I said, but he answered, 'We had a spring in our step, that's how.' This was true.

But I had turned my back on clocks and their inner workings forever. I pointed at a very distant mountain. 'I believe that one to be the crumpled map of Morocco,' I said. He frowned. The map contained another Atlas Range, of course, which in turn was made from the pages of another atlas, large but not quite so enormous. And one of the mountains of that smaller range would also be made from the map of Morocco. An endless cycle had begun. Recursion, smaller and smaller. On one of those mountains my new friend would truly be Atlas and Salta no longer, capable of standing on the summit as a giant and holding the sky on his shoulders, even if it turned out to be a much heavier sky than the one above us now.

I pondered this story and wondered why it was so much longer than the other communications I had received so far. Perhaps because it had been written with the hands of a clock *as well* as with the hand of a shadow rabbit, and clock hands never get tired. They keep going without a rest.

That would explain it neatly, yes indeed. Also the battery in the torch was now dead. It had been drained to its electron dregs. I wondered if these shadows were capable of sucking the light out of the bulbs and whether this particular one had been very greedy.

At any rate I would have to purchase a new battery. In fact I decided to buy a new torch while I was at it. The one I owned was quite old and the on/off switch was loose. And my spare torch had gone missing after the morning of the creation of the shadow rabbit lovers. As it happens, I used the unreliable one a final time before it did break. The result of its malfunction was peculiar and interesting.

Down the stairs I trudged, yawning and rotating my knuckles in the corners of my heavy lidded eyes. The piece of paper contained a grid six rows deep and six columns wide. Each cell of the grid contained words, six words in fact. I was bemused and confused. There is a famous saying in English that a flustered person is "all at sixes and sevens." I was only at sixes as I confronted the hexametric grid.

To hop from dusk to doom	We flop on rugs too soon	Dream of scenes that grow large	Until they seem real and feel	Like the truth when liars weep	Such a sleepy bunny I am
Our eyes shine bright as lamps	In the corner of unlocked rooms	Wishes for the long gone past	Wider than the shields of Sparta	Moons live in buttered skies but	My hutch stands in a pram
While moths circle our fluffy heads	Waiting for absent hugs with sighs	Is the same as never travelling	In the cool airy blue empyrean	Clouds drift like gigantic icy ships	And I am wheeled hither once
Stars gurgle in the old pools	Ignoring the words of the wise	As many times as sighs rise	Light in the darkness of night	Pearly white with a purplish tint	And thither more times than that
No fools would surely ever stoop	To twitch a nose you suppose	High they drift and later fall	Bubbles of trouble pop too soon	And we always hope to hop	On soft pillows and off again
To drink from the liquid sky	Requires a tongue so long fated	That no river thwarted runs dry	Tickle our fingertips in the dusk	Onto the deck with our skates	From pillar to bedpost right away

The damaged on/off switch had caused the torch to repeatedly flash. For a short time, maybe minutes or even only seconds, it would be on, and for a short time it would be off. This stroboscopic effect created and destroyed the shadow rabbit hand many times during the course of the night. Every time it was created it was almost a new being and had the opportunity to write only a few words before it was returned to the oblivion of darkness. The rise and fall of existence and sentience.

At first I thought the small packets of words in the grid were discrete, unlinked to each other, but as I studied them for a long time I realised this simply wasn't so. They *were* connected. It turned out that the grid could be read horizontally across any row, and vertically down any column, and along the main diagonal, and that sensible tales would emerge. There may also be coherent tales on the other diagonals, and semi-coherent ones on a meandering path through the grid. It is a word maze and one may wander where one chooses, into sense or gibberish.

That day I bought a new torch. I also purchased ingredients for food. I thought about what wine to choose, for Belinda was coming to dinner the same evening, then I recalled she never drank wine. So I bought bottles of beer instead. I could have settled for juice or coconut water, but it would be a disaster if she did like beer and I hadn't any for her. I know very little about beer, so I chose the only brand with a name I recognised. I'm not a great cook, but I am adequate and I strived.

She arrived a little late, but what of that? I was delighted to greet her and invite her into my home. She wanted to leave her bicycle outside but I told her to bring it in, just in case. The city is not especially crime ridden but a stolen bicycle isn't ridden at all, at least not by the rightful owner in the wake of its felonious vanishing. She leaned it against the dinner table. I served the vegetable tagine I had prepared, accompanied by flatbreads. I poured her a tall glass of Guinness too.

She laughed at this, sipping it gingerly and saying:

"I rarely drink beer but thanks."

"Ah, my apologies."

"Don't be silly. It was a pleasing thought."

"I hope you'll enjoy the food."

"Already I'm doing so."

We chatted and my nerves evaporated (assuming nerves can do that, I assumed they were solids) and I knew for certain there was a connection between us, and this fact filled me with intense satisfaction. I told her all about the shadow experiments and I showed her some of the texts those bunnies had produced. As she read them, I added, "All I know about the name *Habakkuk* is that he was a prophet."

She answered, "The name of the ice ship probably derives from the famous verse that says, 'I will work a work in your days, which ye will not believe, though it be told you.' At any rate, it seems a perfectly useful name for a massive frozen vessel."

"Yes, I guess it does."

"Nine shadow rabbits have told their tales, in prose, verse and outline. This means there are only three left?"

"You are right. Maybe I ought to make another special effort with the next one. I bought a new torch today."

She examined it curiously. "A Japanese model."

"It looks advanced," I said.

"Will you let me suggest an experimental set up?"

"Please do so, Belinda."

"Why don't you shine the beam of the torch through my glass of beer? The Guinness will act like a prism. The beam that casts the shadow of the rabbit will be flavoured with the drink. Who knows what the result might be? I definitely think it's worth trying."

"So do I," and that's what I did that very night.

I said farewell to Belinda an hour before midnight and watched from the stone steps as she cycled off into a future that I hoped would include us close together in some capacity.

I took the glass of her mostly unfinished beer, positioned it so that the beam of the new torch went right through the black liquid before casting the rabbit's shadow on the wall. Then I retired to bed and in the morning I found a very short text that later in the day I carried with me to Belinda's favourite cafe. Luckily, she was there.

"What do you make of this?" I asked, as I passed the piece of paper to her. And she read the following words:

There was a young hare
from Kildare whose Limericks
were more like haikus.

Which was thought rather rich
at the time because
his haikus did rhyme
and in actual fact were quite fine
or so it said on the news.

My bemused expression elicited a grin from her. "No mystery at all," she said. I asked her to elaborate and she answered, "Your torch is Japanese and you shone it through an Irish beer. Therefore the shadow cast on the wall had some attributes of the former culture and some of the latter. The haiku is a Japanese verse form and the limerick is an Irish one. That's my explanation for this odd poetic fusion."

She was right, undoubtedly. But it now struck me very forcefully that there would only be two more shadow rabbits capable of communicating with our own world. I felt a little sad about this, or perhaps wistful is the better word, for all good things must come to an end, all bad things also, and I was well aware of that immutable truth. When the rabbits no longer left messages for me I would resume my earlier life. More social, friendly and eager to accept invitations to parties.

I decided to ration the appearances of the shadows.

And I resolved that the next time I generated a hand from the shadow of my rabbit, it would be on the second occasion that Belinda came to my dwelling for dinner, which turned out to be one week later. Once again I asked her to bring her bicycle indoors.

She leaned the machine against the dinner table as before, in a slightly different position, and we ate and talked and laughed, and I bathed in the radiance of her smiling eyes, her luminous smile, her glow of health, her aura of a beauty that is part wisdom, part sunshine and part a quality I am utterly unable to define. I basked in Belinda. After dinner she asked me to cast the rabbit's shadow and I was ready with the torch. "Maybe we'll get a result immediately," she remarked.

I admitted it was possible. I positioned the torch and the beam shone through the spokes of her bicycle's back wheel before reaching the rabbit. It seemed that the shadow of the creature, which was a hand, was locked in a prison. The effect was dramatic and we decided not to interfere with it. Then Belinda said, "Why don't we go for a night stroll?" and it was an idea that agreed with my mood. Out we went, walking arm in arm along the riverbank, opposite the university.

"After all," she said, "there's no reason why a shadow should require an entire night to write a poem or story."

"We might just need to absent ourselves for an hour or two," I agreed, but this had never occurred to me before. We were alone on the path for most of the time. A solitary cyclist passed us at low speed, a man with a hat that had huge false ears, rabbit ears. The coincidence made me laugh but was it truly a coincidence? Perhaps it was a cosmic season for things associated with rabbits. Who can tell?

When we returned to my apartment we found that the carrot had been eaten, the shadow pen was empty, and the message was already waiting for us. I picked it up and read it aloud:

d'If you can keep your head when most
        about you
accused of treason have theirs chopped
        off.
d'If you can know you are innocent when
        the judge
and the magistrates doubt all your good
        intentions.
d'If you can wait in a dungeon for
        fourteen years
befriended only by a mad priest called
        Abbe Faria
and learn all sort of useful things from the
        man
and eventually hit the sack without him
        in it.

d'If you can dream of revenge rather than
        carrots;
d'If you can hop and hope for personal
        justice;
d'If you can meet with feral cats and
        weasels
and treat those two impostors just the
        same;
d'If you can find hidden treasure on an
        island
buried there ages ago by some decadent
        prince,
and use the money and jewels to change
        yourself
and adopt a new impressive and suave
        identity:

d'If you can make a mountain of all your
        winnings
and climb to the top only with
        experienced guides,
and fall, and start again right from the
        bottom,
and request no aid from any dedicated
        rescue team.
d'If you can force your better nature and
        your pity
to supress themselves until dark deeds are
        done,
and keep on the trail of those who
        betrayed you
without softening in the slightest your
        inner rage.

d'If you can talk with rascals and remain
        resolute
or lodge with kings nor lose the common
        hutch;
d'If neither dogs nor foxes can enter your
        burrow,
d'If stylish men admire your furry
        birthday suit;
d'If you can fill the enormous warren of
        your life
with a thousand plus pages of adventures
        won,
yours is the Earth and within it. And
        what's more,
you'll be Count Rabbit of Monte Cristo,
        my son!

It was the poem of a fugitive prisoner, for certain! And the shadow of the rabbit was no longer a hand. The rabbit had changed its position and the beam of the torch no longer touched it. The hand was gone, it must have escaped. "I know who he was," I said.

"The prisoner, you mean?" Belinda whispered.

"His name is no secret now."

"Who was he then?"

"Bunnyard Kipling," I replied.

"Oh, I see," she said.

"But not in full."

"In full?" she wondered.

"Bunnyard Kipling Dumas," I declared.

"And he's free at last."

There was nothing more to be said. But I am comfortable with silence and so is Belinda, and it was pleasant enough just to be there with her, no expectations or pressure. We smiled at each other. Then the time came for her to leave and I waved to her as she pedalled in the direction of home. I was already longing for her next visit.

One more rabbit, one more shadow, then the communications would cease. The last message had to be a truly special one, thus arrangements to ensure it was special had to be taken.

I waited for Belinda to accept my third invitation to dinner. She came a few days later. We brought her bicycle indoors but leaned it against the wall farthest from the rabbit. I didn't want to imprison another shadow. It would be unjust. The carrot I gave to the rabbit was the biggest the grocer had ever had in stock. The torch had the most powerful bulb. Everything was ready for a truly impressive finale.

But things didn't go quite as I imagined they would.

That's how life is, of course!

The first aspect that was different from all previous occasions was the fact we observed the process in action. The torch cast the shadow of my rabbit and that shadow looked like a hand. The shadow of the carrot was a pen in that hand. So far, so good.

Then it all went wrong...

This twelfth and last bunny shade had a stronger will than its fellows. It wanted to turn the tables on us. As we watched, the tip of the shadow pen began to glow brighter and brighter.

Then we realised that it wasn't a pen at all but a torch!

The hand turned this torch on us.

We were caught in the beam.

And our shadows were cast onto the wall behind us.

"I'm sorry, Belinda," I said.

"Sorry for what, dear?"

"I have absolutely no idea yet."

"But you feel uneasy?"

"Very. I am sure this rabbit means us harm."

"Let's fight back then!"

I did the only thing I knew how to do well. While Belinda picked up the torch, I raised my hand in front of the beam and used it to create the shape of a rabbit on the wall. My hand's shadow rabbit would cancel out my rabbit's shadow hand. That was the idea. But the enemy hand didn't vanish when Belinda removed the torch.

It remained in place, defined by the all-encompassing glow of its own torch, the torch that had originally been a pen created from the shadow of a carrot. We had lost ultimate control. And now the hand approached my shadow rabbit and seemed to whisper something in its ears. It must have persuaded my rabbit to turn against me.

Suddenly my shadow rabbit nodded and my hand jerked. The rabbit hopped along the wall and my hand followed. I tried to disengage, turn my hand back into a normal hand, but it was stuck. The shadow rabbit was controlling my hand. I was unable to resist. And now the rabbit used its power to cause all sorts of mischief.

As the rabbit capered back and forth, my hand went with it, seized ornaments and flung them on the floor, tore down paintings, yanked the curtains off the rail, turned the table upside down, hurled the chairs into the kitchen, and even began making rude gestures to my beloved. "Help me, Belinda!" I cried, and she took hold of my other hand and pulled me out of the room and up the stairway.

The malign shadow rabbit followed us, sliding up the bannister. We ran into the bedroom, but the rabbit slipped under the door. The attic was the last place to flee. Up the ladder we climbed and through the trapdoor, which we slammed behind us, and the seal was good. Not even a shadow is thin enough to pass through that.

The sounds of commotion came to us in our refuge.

"The house is being destroyed."

"We can't stay here. We will have to climb onto the roof. But it's too high to jump from there. What next?"

We gazed together up at the skylight above us.

It's true I had learned one method of ingenious escape from one of the shadow rabbits, which is to look up at the sky and pretend it is a body of water you are gazing down on, so that any passing cloud of your choice is your reflection, then you are whatever that cloud looks like, a dragon for example, and you can breathe fire and roast your enemies. Then you look up again, wait for a cloud that resembles your original shape and change back. This technique only works when the sky is blue. On overcast days it will fail us, like a ladder without rungs.

It was evening and the sky was a very dark blue.

But it was possible to see clouds.

"Belinda, the skylight is a pond and we are looking into it, so what we see there is our own reflection. Those clouds must be us. But there's only one cloud now, which means that..."

"You and I are just one being. We have fused."

"How strange! How lovely!"

"A gestalt. That's what we are, my dear."

"But what do we *feel* like?"

The cloud that passed overhead was shaped like a carrot. This meant that Belinda and I together were a carrot. But it didn't feel that way at all. Then the cloud changed its form into a fox with a bushy tail. No, it still wasn't quite right. It changed again, into a ship made of ice sailing seas too warm, and it began to melt. We began to melt. If we melted away we would escape the rabbit below, but would it be the end for us? Before it melted, the cloud briefly assumed the shape of a hand, a human hand, and we decided to seize the opportunity.

We opened the trapdoor and descended the ladder.

Giant hands are good at climbing.

The shadow rabbit panicked when it saw us and bounded out of the bedroom and down the stairs. When we reached the living room, all was in darkness. The glowing tip of the carrot torch had been nibbled away. The real bunny had already devoured it.

"This means there is no twelfth message," I said.

Belinda approached the sheet of paper and picked it up. "No, there is one," she said, "and it seems interesting."

We studied it together. It was a story, structured in an unusual way. The sentences were of precise length and the number of words of each sentence were tagged onto their ends.

(0). Taxis (1). Night (1). Safe travel (2). Better that way (3). It was just before dawn (5). Almost certainly the hardest time to catch one (8). I am an ethical individual and I insist on always catching them humanely (13). I flagged one down as it passed and I told the driver to take me to a location one mile away (21). He grumbled a little because it was such a short distance and yet he accepted me as a passenger because a taxi driver who refuses a fare is a fool and everyone knows it (34). We trundled along the dark road and only the eyes of an occasional owl in the gnarled trees provided any light at all in that very lonely place and I didn't try to engage in conversation with the driver but remained on one of the back seats wrapped in the silence of my profound thoughts (55). These thoughts consisted of a review of my life to date and how a rabbit such as myself had always struggled to be successful in a world of human beings and yet there was no bitterness in my heart despite all my tribulations because I had found a method of striking back at those who had tormented me for so long and it consisted of catching taxis but always humanely and taking them one mile away from where they had been caught and releasing them back into the wild (89). The 'wild' part of the process comes from the taxi drivers going wild when the passenger simply hops away instead of paying and now I saw we were almost at the destination and I prepared to open the door and flee as soon as the taxi stopped but much to my surprise I realised that there was a thing standing by the side of the road just where the taxi was due to pull over and this thing was of an unimaginable shape and substance and the only way I was able to focus on it was by rapidly blinking my eyes and it was clear the driver was feeling nervous too because he muttered the word 'alien' as he applied the brakes and when the thing stepped forward and the driver said 'where to?' the new passenger merely pointed at the night sky (144).

"Are you thinking what I'm thinking?"

Belinda nodded. "The first twelve numbers of the Fibonacci sequence. Twelve rabbits, so it all fits, only I don't know how it fits, or why. Maybe we weren't ever supposed to know."

"And it was rabbits that gave Fibonacci the idea for his number series in the first place. He asked himself how many pairs of rabbits would be in a field after one year if the field only had one pair to start with. Twelve months in one year and if the rabbits produce a new pair every month, the answer works out as 144. The final sentence in the final message from the last shadow has that many words in it."

"It is late now. Maybe too late for me to cycle home."

"I have a spare bedroom," I said.

"That's good," she replied.

Before we retired for the night, I pondered.

"The twelfth rabbit cast our shadows on the wall with its carrot torch. I wonder what those shadow looked like?"

"No need to wonder," Belinda said, "they're still there."

I turned to frown at the sight.

The carrot torch must have been quite different from ordinary torches because it had etched our outlines into the plaster of the wall. Belinda and I were frozen there, our silhouettes dominating the wall, looming like the paintings inside the temples of some hitherto undiscovered civilisation. I admired them for a few moments with a pleasure mingled with disquiet. It seemed an augur of a dramatic event.

Then something else happened.

I had been expecting it ever since my conversation with Belinda when she span the wheels of her bicycle and projected a shadow onto the white cards threaded through the spokes.

A rabbit is an animal. The shadow of a rabbit is a hand, the hand of a different animal, the hand of a human being. A human being is an animal. Therefore the shadow of a human is a hand, the hand of a different being, the hand of an alien entity. If I make a rabbit with my hand and then stop making it, the rabbit turns back into a hand. If the aliens who are making us with their hands stop making us, we will turn back into *their* hands. At this very instant, that's what they did.

Belinda is one hand now and I am another.

We are a pair of hands that belong to the same unimaginable cosmic lifeform, and although we are its hands we are unable to even guess what that organism looks like. Our lives have changed a lot as a consequence, but it's really not as bad as it sounds.

There are always compensations. We still hug tightly, an embrace that is actually two alien hands clutching each other. And when those hands pray to an alien god, we are pressed together in love, in an act of worship that is also the answer to our prayers.